This edition published by Parragon Books Ltd in 2013

Parragon Books Ltd
Chartist House
15–17 Trim Street
Bath BA1 1HA, UK
www.parragon.com

ISBN 978-1-78186-600-9

Printed in China

Peter Pan

Return to Never Land

Bath • New York • Singapore • Hong Kong • Cologne • Delhi
Melbourne • Amsterdam • Johannesburg • Shenzhen

High in the sky, Peter Pan and Tinker Bell
sailed off through the clouds to Never Land.
"Good-bye, Wendy!" Peter Pan shouted.
"I'll always believe in you, Peter Pan!" Wendy called back.

That was how Wendy, now all grown up, always ended the story. Her son, Danny, never got tired of hearing about his mother's adventures with Peter Pan and the Lost Boys.

But Wendy's daughter, Jane, didn't have time for childish things. There was a war going on and Jane had promised her father that she would take care of the family while he was away.

When Jane found out she was supposed to go somewhere safe until the war was over, she was angry.

"I'm not going!" she argued.

"We'll be together again," Wendy told her. "You must have faith."

"Faith, trust, pixie dust. Mother, those are just words from your stories." Jane stomped over to the window. "They don't mean anything. Peter Pan isn't real and people don't fly!"

It was all too much for Jane. She lay down on the window seat and cried herself to sleep.

A noise woke Jane in the middle of the night. She gasped.
Standing over her was – could it be? – Captain Hook!

"Hello, Wendy," he said, mistaking Jane for her mother.

Before Jane could say a word, Hook's first mate, Mr Smee,
stuffed her into a sack. They boarded Hook's flying pirate
ship and set sail for the second star to the right and straight
on till morning. They were going to Never Land!

When the boat anchored, Jane peeked out of the sack and
watched the pirates.

"With Wendy as bait, we shall lure Peter Pan to his
doom!" snarled Captain Hook. "Summon the beast!"

Smee dumped a bucket of fish over the side of the boat.
Suddenly, a giant octopus rose to gobble up the fish!

Just then, a shadow appeared behind the topsail. The sail was sliced open with a dagger – and there was Peter Pan!

"I've a little something for you," Captain Hook said to him. "A certain friend of yours – Wendy!"

Hook dropped the sack and it plunged down toward the hungry octopus. Peter Pan dove after it.

"I did it!" Captain Hook said. "I'm free of Peter Pan forever!"

Peter flew to a nearby rock and freed Jane from the sack. "You're sure not Wendy," he said.

Jane gasped. Peter Pan and Tinker Bell were floating right before her eyes!

"Oh, I get it," she said. "I'm dreaming. You're not real."

Then Jane explained that she was Wendy's daughter. Peter could hardly believe it.

Peter Pan took Jane to meet the Lost Boys.
"Boys, this is Jane!" said Peter. "She's gonna stay here and
be our new mother and tell us stories."

Jane shook her head. "Actually, I'm afraid I'm not
very good at telling stories," she said. "I have to go home."
But the only way Jane could go home was to fly. And the
only way to fly was with faith, trust and pixie dust. Jane
didn't believe in any of that. Peter tried to help her by giving
her a push, but she kept falling and crashing into things.

Jane soon became frustrated by the Lost Boys' silly games and stormed off. Tinker Bell followed her and pulled her hair.

"Leave me alone!" Jane cried. "I don't believe in any of this – and I especially don't believe in fairies!"

Suddenly, Tinker Bell's light began to fade. If Jane didn't believe in fairies, Tinker Bell's light would go out forever!

Meanwhile, Captain Hook had a truly evil plan.

He found Jane and lied to her, telling her he wished he could take them both home on his flying ship.

"But Peter stole my treasure and my men would mutiny if I so much as tried to leave without it," Hook said, pretending to cry. He promised Jane a ride home if she helped him. Hook also promised not to hurt Peter Pan. Then he gave Jane a whistle to blow when she found the treasure.

The Lost Boys were happy to see Jane again. They took her on a wild adventure through Never Land.

Jane had a wonderful time! She forgot all about her responsibilities and being grown-up.

Peter said they'd do anything for her. "Why don't we play a game, like maybe. . . Treasure Hunt?" Jane suggested.

Everyone started to search. Jane walked into Dead Man's
Cave. And there, right before her eyes, was Hook's treasure!

Peter Pan was so impressed that Jane had found the
treasure, he proclaimed her the very first Lost Girl. Jane
was very happy! She threw the whistle away and decided
she would never tell Hook about the treasure.

But one of the Lost Boys found the whistle – and he blew it!

In an instant, Captain Hook and his pirates appeared. They captured Peter Pan and the Lost Boys and chained them up. "Stop it! Please!" Jane shouted.

Jane tried to explain to Peter that Captain Hook had tricked her. But Peter would not listen. "You lied to me and because you don't believe in fairies, Tink's light is going out!" he cried.

There wasn't a moment to lose! Jane ran as fast as she could to Tinker Bell's house. She knelt beside the fairy. "This is all my fault. I'm so sorry," Jane said. She started to cry.

Suddenly, Tinker Bell's light began to flicker back to life! Jane did believe!

Back on Hook's pirate ship, the Lost Boys stood locked and chained to the mast. Captain Hook was about to make Peter Pan walk the plank!

"Say your prayers, Peter Pan!" Captain Hook said with an evil laugh.

"Not so fast, you old codfish!" said a voice. It was Jane – and Tinker Bell was at her side!

"Jane!" cried Peter. "Tinker Bell, you're alive!"

Jane snatched a dagger from a pirate and the key
from Hook and freed Peter Pan and the Lost Boys.
Armed with slingshots, the Lost Boys began shooting
jewels from Hook's treasure overboard. Diamonds, rubies
and emeralds splashed into the sea.

"Gimme that!" the pirates shouted, jumping into the
water after the jewels.

Hook thought he had Jane trapped on top of the mast.
"Give up, girl!" the villain snarled.
"Never!" cried Jane. And thanks to a little faith, trust and
pixie dust, she flew out of Hook's grasp. All the pirates and
their captain ended up bobbing in the ocean with the
hungry octopus!
The Lost Boys – and Girl – had defeated Captain Hook!

Peter Pan, Tinker Bell and Jane flew home to London. While Jane told Danny all about her grand adventures, Wendy cautiously approached the window and peered out. Would she really see Peter Pan again?

"Peter?" she whispered. And there he was.

"You've changed," said Peter.

"Not really," Wendy said. "Not ever."

Suddenly, there was a knock at the door. Jane's father was home! As the happy family reunited, Peter Pan and Tinker Bell flew off to the second star on the right. . . and headed straight on till morning.